TREEHOUSE
RESCUE!

PUFFIN

Map of my woods

This is a map of the woods where I live. You can see who else lives here too. It's in my dad's journal which I always have with me.

ROCKY ISLAND

OLD BROWN'S ISLAND

Old Brown is very bad tempered. We stay away from him.

MR JEREMY FISHER'S POND

SQUIRREL NUTKIN'S WOOD

MRS TIGGYWINKLE'S LAUNDRY

Squirrel Nutkin has some of the best, and, nuttiest, ideas.

One sunny morning, Peter, Lily and Benjamin were hopping happily through the woods. Suddenly Peter stopped, sniffed and rubbed his chin . . .

"Someone's following us!"

Peter spun round, then stood still as a statue.
Behind him, Benjamin and Lily trembled with fear.
"Don't worry," said Peter. "We'll all stick
together."

"Hello, my floppy-eared friends," hissed Mr Tod, licking his lips.

"MMM! Perfect for a PIE!"

"Quick. Let's hide!" called Peter, dodging Mr Tod and bounding away.

The friends hopped and hopped then stopped when Benjamin heard giggling in the trees.

"Lucky squirrels! It's easy to hide up there."

"Yes, it is. Great idea, Benjamin!" said Peter.
"If we had a hideout in the Squirrel Camp,
Mr Tod would NEVER find us."

The Camp was VERY high up. Benjamin did NOT enjoy the journey.

Squirrel Nutkin was bouncing around in the branches. He was not at all sure rabbits belonged in trees. "You can't just HAVE a hideout up here," he squeaked importantly.

"First you have to pass three SECRET SQUIRREL TESTS."

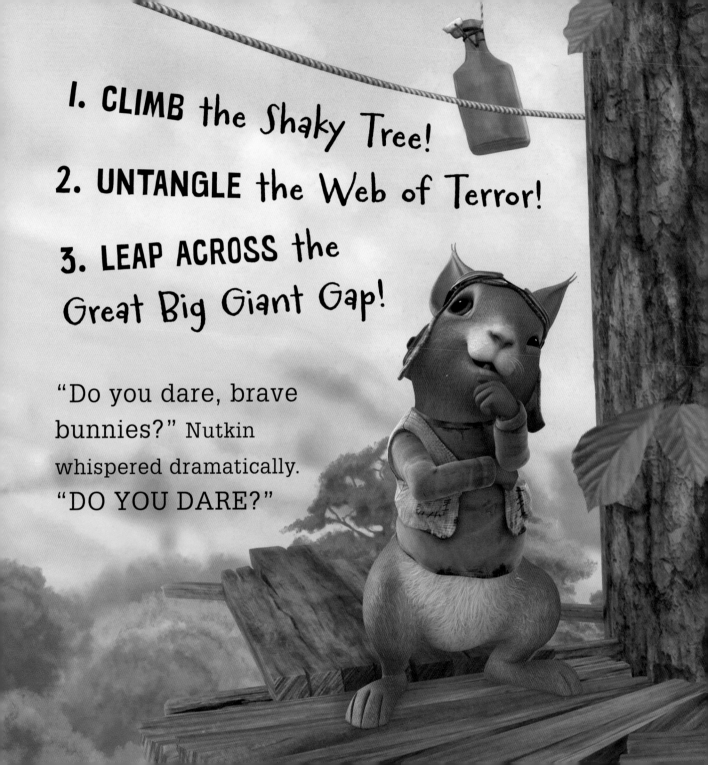

1. **CLIMB** the Shaky Tree!

2. **UNTANGLE** the Web of Terror!

3. **LEAP ACROSS** the Great Big Giant Gap!

"Do you dare, brave bunnies?" Nutkin whispered dramatically. "DO YOU DARE?"

The brave bunnies DID dare.

Benjamin made it up to
the top of the Shaky Tree
. . . and shook with terror.

"Pass!"

"Well done,
Benjamin!"

Lily tiptoed through the tangled Web of Terror.

"I can do this," Lily murmured to herself.

And she was right!

"Pass!"

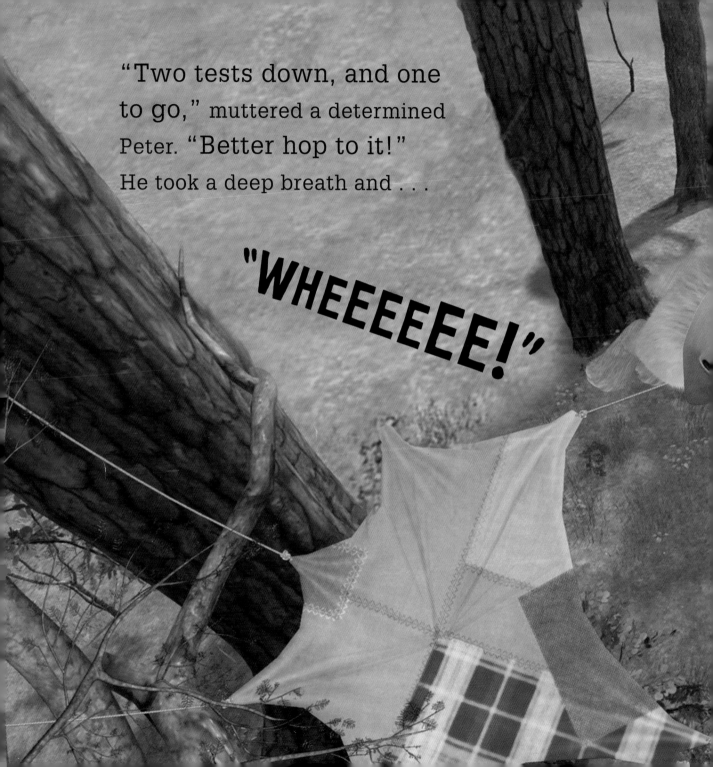

"Two tests down, and one to go," muttered a determined Peter. "Better hop to it!"
He took a deep breath and . . .

"WHEEEEEE!"

"Hopping hazelnuts!"

gasped Nutkin.

"Final test . . .

. . . failed!"

The Great Big Giant Gap was just TOO BIG. "Oh, no!" sighed Peter. Luckily, the giggly squirrels caught him in their bucket as he fell, and winched him back up.

There was to be no treehouse hideout after all.

The three friends made their way sadly down to the ground in the lift.

"At least we won't have to listen to those squawking squirrels every day," Lily sighed.

"And it is AWFULLY high up," added Benjamin.

Suddenly the wood was filled with a terrifying SCREECHING sound . . .

The noise coming from the Squirrel Camp had woken Old Brown, a rather crotchety owl.

Old Brown did NOT think highly of silly, noisy squirrels.

Nutkin ran for his life!

"Old Brown is attacking
the Squirrel Camp!" yelled Peter.

"We have to get back
up there and help!"

Nutkin was trapped high in the trees
on the other side of the Great Big Giant Gap.

"I've got a plan!" said Peter.
"It's risky but it might just work."

Dodging panicking squirrels one
way and Old Brown's needle-sharp
talons the other, he and brave
Benjamin . . . GRABBED
Nutkin's paw . . .

and **SWUNG** across
the Great Big
Giant Gap . . .

. . . just in time.

The rabbits watched as Nutkin's assistant chalked
a big tick beside the final Squirrel Test.

"Pass!"

"Look at that!"
laughed Peter.
"Maybe rabbits
DO belong in
trees after all!"

Mr Tod spent the rest of the day looking for rabbits, and blaming squirrels for the hazelnuts that showered down upon his beautiful velvet coat.

"Those confounded squirrels!"

The friends felt safe at last . . .

. . . in their new secret clubhouse.

"This is what I call a good
hiding place!" laughed Peter.

"It's the perfect spot
to plan new ADVENTURES!"

OUR TREETOP HIDEOUT

Rabbits can't climb trees like squirrels, so we travel up and down in this lift. Only the squirrels really know how it works, but it's better than brilliant!

Up to Branch Manager's office

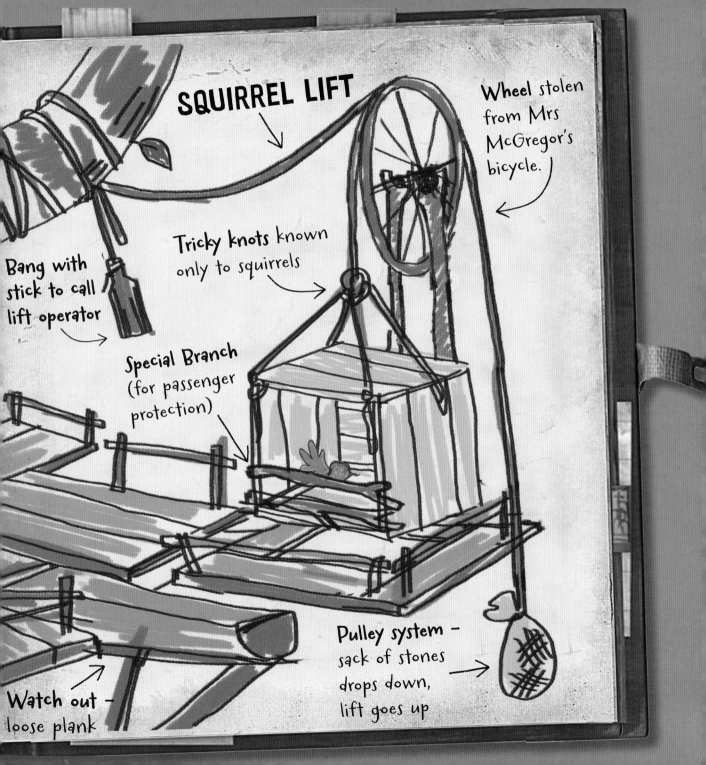

Let's work on your **WOBBLE!**

Today we're practising our balancing skills. It's fun doing things together and we'd love it if you joined in too. It's tricky for rabbits as we've got BIG FEET!

Good balance is important in the sky-high Squirrel Camp!

Benjamin and Lily passed their Squirrel Tests with flying colours.

WHY DON'T YOU TRY THESE?

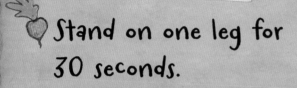 Stand on one leg for 30 seconds.

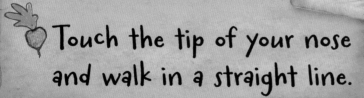 Walk along a low wall, or a fallen log. (Hold on tight to a grown-up's hand.)

Touch the tip of your nose and walk in a straight line.

Awesome skills, my friend!

CONGRATULATIONS!
SKILL IN BALANCING CERTIFICATE

Awarded to

Ben and Abbie

Johnsons

Age

6 and 3

Squirrel Nutkin

SQUIRREL NUTKIN
BEST BALANCER IN THE WOOD

PR CLUB